This Little Tiger book belongs to:

_____

_____

_____

For Heather,
Erin and Isaac
— A B

VISIT
GOLDEN
DODO
ZOO
TODAY

LITTLE TIGER PRESS LTD,
an imprint of the
Little Tiger Group
1 Coda Studios,
189 Munster Road, London SW6 6AW
www.littletiger.co.uk

First published in Great Britain 2014
This edition published 2019

Text and illustrations copyright © Alison Brown 2014
Alison Brown has asserted her right to be identified
as the author and illustrator of this work under
the Copyright, Designs and Patents Act, 1988

A CIP catalogue record for this book is available
from the British Library

Mighty Mo

Alison Brown

LITTLE TIGER

LONDON

Mo was bored.

Bored, bored, bored.

"There must be
SOMETHING
amazing I can do,"
Mo said.

Ernestine was making
incredible ice creams.
"That's IT!" cried Mo.
"I can do that!"

"I'll be MARVELLOUS Mo – King of Sprinkles!"

"Triple Whippy, coming up!"

sNAp

"Hmm. Maybe I should try something else amazing."

Alphonse was brilliant with balloons.

"I can do **THAT**. They'll call me

MAGNIFICENT *mo*
– POWer-puffer!"

"OOPS!"

"Oh NO, NO, No! Ho, Ho, Too MUCH Puff!"

At last Mo found the PERFECT thing.

"Now this looks totally fabulous!" he said.

"I'll be Mo the Majestic – HAIRDO HERO!"

"I'm not coming out again. EVER!"

"Don't give up, Mo," said his friends. "You'll find SOMETHING SPECIAL to do!" Just at that moment they heard a commotion . . .

"What's the panic, Percival?" asked Mo.
"Big Ron has stolen the Golden Dodo!"
Percival squeaked. "We need YOU, Mo!"

"ME? Why me?"

"You're **super-strong!** You're **super-fast!**" cried Percival. "Only YOU can catch Big Ron!"

"Fantastic!" said Mo. "At last! Something amazing I can do!"

"Hey you, not so fast!"

"Come back, you big striped sardine!"

"This calls for something REALLY spectacular ..."

OTCHA!"

"Put me down!"
Big Ron yelled.

And so Mo did
just that . . .

. . right into a BIG pile of elephant poo!

"My lovely robbery - RUINED!" Big Ron blubbed.

"You're nothing but a rotten raccoon!"

Mo smiled. "I'm not just ANY raccoon . . ." he said. "I'm Mo . . ."

"... the **MARVELLOUS**, the **MAGNIF**